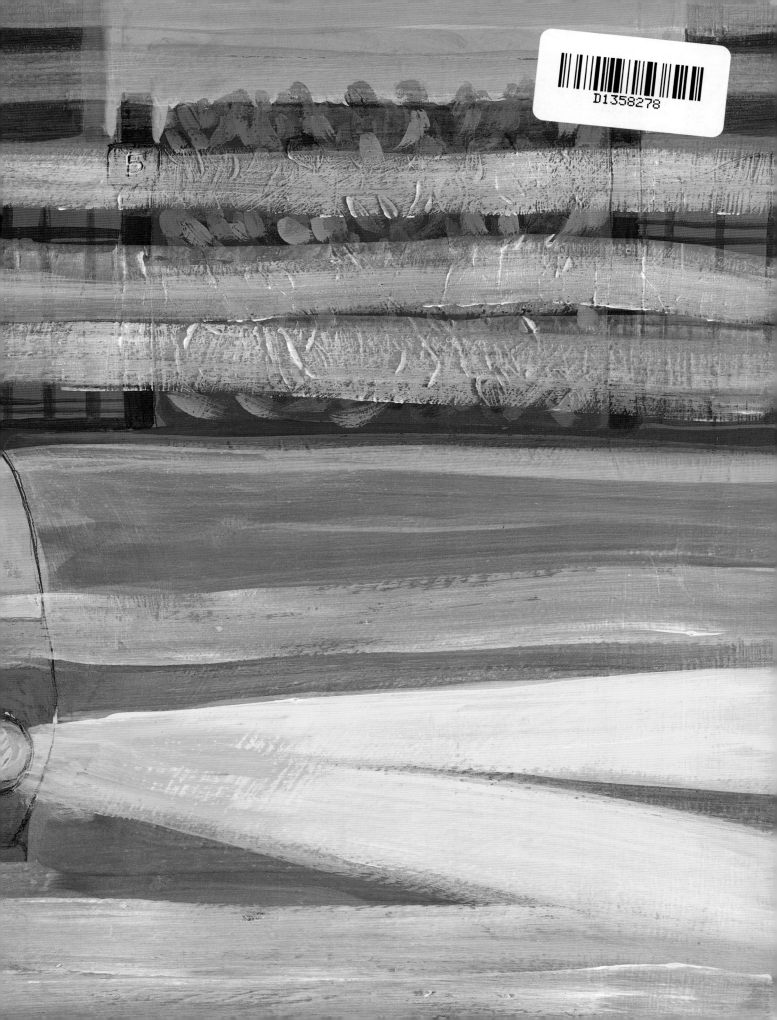

To Carlo,
　　my twin brother
　　　　—F. C.

Published by Bloomsbury U.S.A. Children's Books
175 Fifth Avenue, New York, NY 10010
Distributed to the trade by Holtzbrinck Publishers

Library of Congress Cataloging-in-Publication Data
Chessa, Francesca.
The mysterious package / by Francesca Chessa. — 1st U.S. ed.
p.　　cm.
Summary: When an enormous package is delivered to their house,
Charlie and Frances try to determine what could be inside.
ISBN-13: 978-1-59990-028-5 • ISBN-10: 1-59990-028-9
[1. Brothers and sisters—Fiction. 2. Family life—Fiction.] I. Title.
PZ7.C425224Mys 2007　　　　[E]—dc22　　　　2006023134

First U.S. Edition 2007
Printed in China
10 9 8 7 6 5 4 3 2 1

The Mysterious Package

by FRANCESCA CHESSA

BLOOMSBURY
CHILDREN'S
BOOKS

It was a very foggy day and Charlie and Frances were arguing, as usual, about the game they were playing. Suddenly, the doorbell rang . . .

"A package has come!" shouted Mom.

"It's very big!" yelled Charlie and Frances.

"It must be a present for me," said Charlie. "It could be a very **big car!**"

"It's not a car," said Frances. "It's a **speedy scooter** for me!"

They both wanted the package so badly that
they started arguing again.

"It's mine!" shouted Frances.

"No, it's mine!" cried Charlie.

"Mom, who is that present for?"
they asked together.
"It's a surprise," said Mom. "We have to wait for
Daddy to get home before we can open it."

"If we have to wait for Daddy, then it's definitely something dangerous," said Charlie. "Maybe it's a lion!"
"That's impossible. We'd be able to hear him roar!" said Frances.

"But listen!" said Charlie. "You can hear something like a heartbeat."
"Yes," said Frances. "Maybe the lion isn't roaring because he's fast asleep."

"We will have **SO** much fun together."

"If there **is** a lion in there, then he's **mine!**" said Frances.

"I'll be fearless
in the night
and we
can sit
and watch the stars
together."

And they both wanted the lion so badly that
they started arguing again.

"It's mine!" shouted Frances.

"No, it's mine!" cried Charlie.

At last, Daddy came home.

"Daddy! Please tell us what's inside the package," Charlie and Frances said together.

"But this isn't my package!" said Daddy.
"The package I'm waiting for is much
smaller than this one."

"Oh, no!" thought
Charlie and Frances.
"Maybe the lion is not for us."

Just then, the
doorbell rang.

It was the delivery man again. "I'm sorry, sir. I delivered that package to the wrong address this morning. This big package is for Mr. Red, who lives next door. Here's *your* package."

"Great!" said Daddy. "My new tool kit!"

"Hmph! But what can we do with a tool kit?" asked Charlie.

"I know!" said Frances. "I've got a great idea."

"Daddy! We need your tool kit ...,"

they shouted together,

". . . to build a very big house for the *next* lion that gets delivered!"

And Charlie
and Frances
didn't argue once.